Fun with GRAMMAR
Book 1

MOONSTONE

Published in Moonstone
by Rupa Publications India Pvt. Ltd 2023
7/16, Ansari Road, Daryaganj
New Delhi 110002

Sales centres:
Prayagraj Bengaluru Chennai
Hyderabad Jaipur Kathmandu
Kolkata Mumbai

P-ISBN: 978-93-5702-331-3
E-ISBN: 978-93-5702-329-0

First impression 2023

10 9 8 7 6 5 4 3 2 1

Printed in India

CONTENTS

THE ENGLISH ALPHABET

Let's Learn

Let us have a look at the capital and small letters.

Capital Letters

A	B	C	D	E
F	G	H	I	J
K	L	M	N	O
P	Q	R	S	T
U	V	W	X	Y
		Z		

Small Letters

a	b	c	d	e
f	g	h	i	j
k	l	m	n	o
p	q	r	s	t
u	v	w	x	y
		z		

The English alphabet has a set of 26 letters. The letters are written in two forms: capital letters and small letters.

The capital letters are also called upper-case letters.

The small letters are also called lower-case letters.

A **Write the small letter next to each capital letter.**

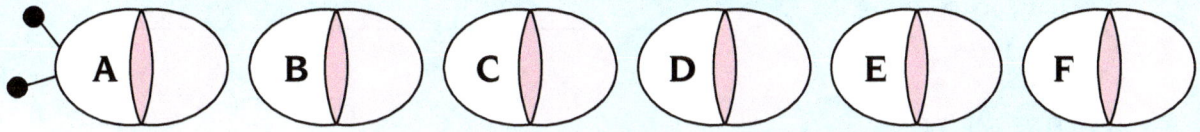

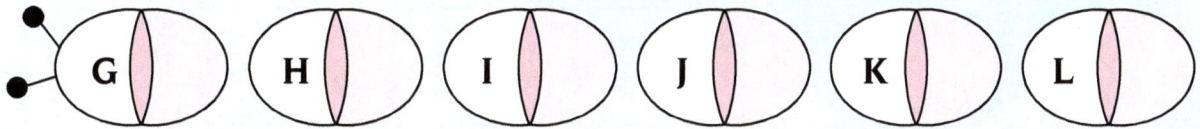

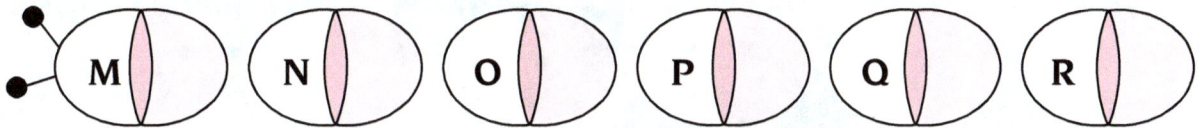

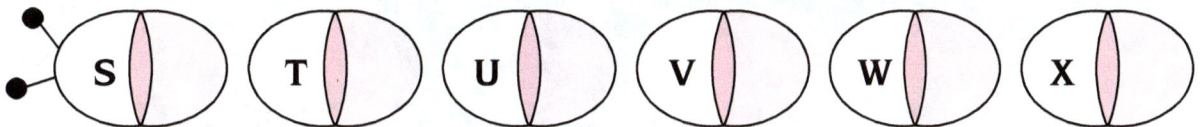

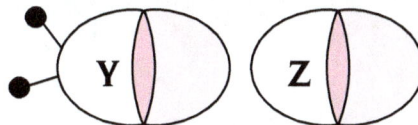

A | B | C | D | E | F |

G | H | I | J | K | L |

M | N | O | P | Q | R |

S | T | U | V | W | X |

Y | Z |

The English alphabet is written in alphabetical order from A to Z.

The above activity follows the correct alphabetical order in upper and lower cases.

B **Members of the Family.**

Your Name   :   _____

Father's Name   :   _____

Mother's Name   :   _____

Friend's Name   :   _____

Rewrite and arrange the letters of these names in alphabetical order.

Your Name   :   _____

Father's Name   :   _____

Mother's Name   :   _____

Friend's Name   :   _____

Five Vowels

a	b	c	d	e	f	g	h	i	j	k	l	m
n	o	p	q	r	s	t	u	v	w	x	y	z

In the above letters, the letters **a, e, i, o, u** are special letters. They are called **Vowels**. There are five vowels in the English alphabet.

The other letters are called **Consonants**.

C **Fill in the vowels (a, e, i, o, u) to complete the names.**

t _ p	s _ n	_ w l
c _ p	d _ g	t _ n
n _ p	l _ p	_ n t
b _ n	m _ g	r _ d
h _ n	c _ w	g _ n
p _ n	v _ n	b _ d
b _ rd	j _ mp	b _ ll
b _ wl	c l _ p	p _ ck

Let's Revise

There are 26 letters in the English language.

They can be written in small or capital letters.

The letters **a**, **e**, **i**, **o**, **u** are called **vowels**.

The other letters are called **consonants**.

Let's Do

D **Arrange the names of animals in alphabetical order.**

- Hen
- Pig
- Cat
- Dog

- Zebra
- Alligator
- Sheep
- Frog

- Bird
- Duck
- Crocodile
- Horse

- Buffalo
- Tiger
- Lion

....

....

....

....

....

E Circle the right picture for each word.

A FAN

A CAT

A CAR

A BOOK

NOUNS

Read the given story.

Momo and Bora

Momo and Bora were good friends. One day, Momo made some bread and snacks. He said, "We are going on a trip. Eat well now. Our next meal will only be at night." Momo started eating the snacks. Bora said, "I don't like these snacks, they are not tasty." Bora did not eat the food. They started the trip. On the way, Bora began to get hungry. In the forest, he only found fruits such as apples, bananas and oranges that had fallen on the ground. He ate them.

Bora realised that everything tastes good when one is hungry.

Look at the underlined words. The words Bora, Momo, snacks, bread, apples, bananas, oranges, fruits, trip, night etc. are all names. They are names of people, places, and things. All such words that denote names are called **Naming Words**.

> **Naming words are called NOUNS**

Read out the names of the children.

Tony

David

Ruby   Mary

Joseph

Sunny

Tony, Ruby, David, Mary, Joseph, Sunny, and many more such names of people are nouns.

> **Names of people or persons are called NOUNS**

A **Identify the nouns in the following sentences.**

1. Soni is a good girl.

2. I like Robby.

3. Sam lives near my house.

4. Danny is my friend.

5. Nancy loves ice-cream.

Read the names of things given in the box below.

Names of things in a room:

BED   TELEVISION   CHAIR   CLOSET   MAT

Names of things in the school –

BENCH   BOARD   GROUND   CHALK   TABLE

Names of things on the road:

CAR   BUS   SIGNAL   FOOTPATH   SHOP

Names of things in the park:

TREE   FLOWER   PLANT   GATE   ROCK

The names in the above boxes are things that we find all around us.
All these things have a name.

Names of ALL THINGS are called NOUNS

B   Write the names of things in the box.

Name things that we eat / drink:

....

Name things in the bag:

....

Name things that we travel by:

....

Name things that we wear:

....

Read the names of PLACES mentioned below.

School

Restaurant

Church

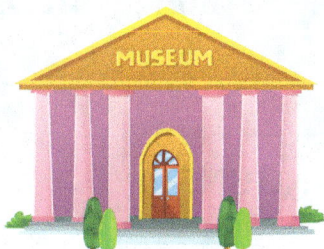

Museum

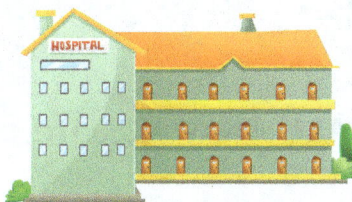

Hospital

Park

Words that name a place are called Nouns. The names of places such as police station, house, school, park, store, apartment, hospital, farm, factory, kitchen, classroom, Delhi, India, and Egypt, etc., are all called Nouns.

> **Names of ALL PLACES are called NOUNS**

C **Fill in the blanks with the names of PLACES mentioned in the box.**

1. The trees are in the _____.

2. The children go to _____ daily.

3. I bought my shoes from a _____.

4. The sick are in the _____.

5. We read books in the _____.

Library

Park

School

Hospital

Shop

13

Read the following paragraph and see the underlined words.

Last Sunday, Karan and his family went to the zoo. The weather was nice and clear. In the zoo, they saw many different types of <u>animals</u>. They first saw an <u>elephant</u> with a long trunk. Karan and his sister were very happy. Then, they saw a <u>giraffe</u>, <u>lion</u>, <u>monkey</u>, <u>deer</u>, and <u>leopard</u>. Moving ahead, they saw other animals such as <u>hippopotamus</u>, <u>crocodile</u> and <u>tortoise</u>. The family spent the day in enjoyment.

The underlined words 'crocodile', 'elephant', 'deer', 'lion', 'tortoise', etc., are names of animals.

> **Names of ALL ANIMALS are called NOUNS**

D **Fill in the blanks with the correct name of the animal given in the box.**

DUCK	CAT	OCTOPUS	HEN	GIRAFFE
COW	LION	TIGER	DOG	ELEPHANT

1. The _____ gives us milk.

2. A _____ has a long neck.

3. A _____ gives eggs.

4. A _____ has a mane.

5. The _____ says meow.

6. A _____ barks.

7. The _____ has a trunk.

8. The _____ is the king of the jungle.

9. An _____ has eight legs.

10. A _____ says quack-quack.

More than One

When there are two or more of something, it is considered plural.

A pumpkin

A turtle

A doll

Three pumpkins

Four turtles

Three dolls

A noun can be used for more than one thing, such as a person, animal, or place. We can add an 's' at the end of the word to mean more than one.

E   **Add an 's' to the end of the word to form its plural.**

1.   Apple- _____   2.   Ball- _____

3.   Plate- _____   4.   Frog- _____

5.   Book- _____   6.   Tree- _____

7.   House- _____   8.   Toy- _____

9.   Bag- _____   10.   Bird- _____

COUNTABLE NOUNS AND UNCOUNTABLE NOUNS

Look at the following items. Can you count them?

How many bananas are there?

How many apples are there?

Can you count juice in the glass?

We can count banana and apples, but we cannot count juice.

Countable nouns (or count **nouns**) are those that refer to something that can be counted. **They have both singular and plural forms.**

Examples: cat/cats; woman/women; country/countries.

Uncountable Nouns are those that refer to things that cannot be counted **and so they do not regularly have a plural form.**

Examples: rain, flour, earth, wine, or wood

Uncountable nouns can't be preceded by **a** or **an**.

We can make uncountable things countable.

We cannot count water but this is the way to make water countable.

There are **three pails** of water.

> When we collect uncountable nouns and put them into containers, we can count containers.

Example:

a spoonful of salt

a glass of milk

a cup of tea

17

A From the chart below, identify which nouns are countable and which are uncountable? Write them under the correct heading.

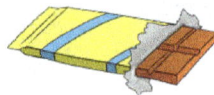

Countable   Uncountable

_____   _____

_____   _____

_____   _____

_____   _____

_____   _____

_____   _____

B Fill in the blanks with suitable uncountable nouns. Pick the words from the word bank given below.

salt	smoke	money	milk	luggage
cereals	hair	health	electricity	air

1. He loves to eat _____ in the morning.

2. Her _____ was long when she went to the hairdresser. Now it is short.

3. _____ is hard to earn. Spend it wisely.

4. We sprinkle _____ on food to make it tastier, but we must not use too much of it.

5. We add _____ to coffee if we do not want black coffee.

6. There is not enough _____ in the tyre.

7. _____ filled the room when the grass was burning outside.

8. Your _____ looks heavy.

9. Please take good care of your _____.

10. We have no _____ today due to a power failure.

C Fill in the blanks with a, an or some.

1. Would you like to have _____ coffee?

2. Do you want _____ paper or _____ pen?

3. Would you like to eat _____ apple or _____ mango?

4. I want _____ butter on my toast.

5. We need _____ glue to fix this vase.

19

6. My father drinks _____ big glass of milk every morning.

7. There is _____ orange on the table.

8. There are _____ beautiful flowers in the garden.

9. There is _____ old man on the counter.

10. The dog has _____ bone in his mouth.

D Is the underlined noun countable or uncountable?

1. The children fell asleep quickly after a busy day of fun. _____

2. I don't have much hair. _____

3. I thought I heard a noise. _____

4. Have you got some paper? _____

5. Our house has seven rooms. _____

6. Is there room for me to sit here? _____

7. We like large bottles of mineral water. _____

8. My mother uses real butter in the cakes she bakes. _____

9. Have you got time for a cup of coffee? _____

10. How many politicians does it take to pass a simple law? _____

11. Most kids like milk, but Joey hates it. _____

12. Most pottery is made of clay. _____

13. Michael can play several different musical instruments. _____

14. I was feeling so stressed that I ate an entire box of cookies. _____

Person

Place

What is a noun?

Animal

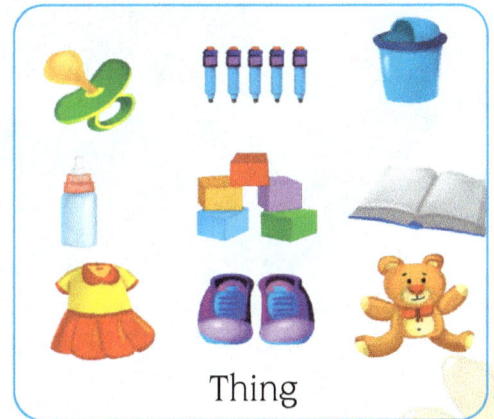

Thing

Let's Do

A **Circle the words that are nouns.**

run	cat	house	sleep	happy
book	tree	car	eat	lunch
foot	apple	sad	cry	cow
see	pan	dog	jump	hand

B **Use the nouns to complete the sentences below.**

book	monkey	bus	pig	ball
song	pencil	table	finger	room

1. I use a _____ to draw a picture.

2. Every night, we read a _____ together in bed.

3. The dirty little _____ played in the mud.

4. He put the plate on the _____.

5. We go to school by _____.

6. John cut his _____ with a sharp knife.

7. The _____ ate a banana.

8. My kitty likes to play with a _____.

9. My sister sang a _____.

10. I want to paint my _____ blue.

ARTICLES

English has three articles: *A, AN,* and *THE.* These articles are used before nouns to show whether the nouns are general or specific.

The **definite article: the,** is used before a noun to indicate that the noun is known to the reader. **The indefinite articles: a an,** are used before a noun that is general or not known.

For example:

• I bought **a** blue sweater yesterday.

• I bought **an** apple and an orange. **The** apple was delicious.

A **Underline the correct article (a / an / the) in each sentence:**

1. John wanted to read a / an comic book so he went to the / a super comic store.

2. The / A church on the corner is progressive.

3. Lisa put a / an orange on her yogurt.

4. The class went on a / an field trip.

5. I borrowed an / a pencil from your pencil box.

6. Marriam likes to read an / the short stories.

7. Monday is the / a first day of an / the week.

8. I saw a / an elephant at the zoo.

9. Pam quickly ate the / an pizza as she was hungry.

10. The dog caught a / an stick.

B Complete the following sentences with A, AN or THE:

1. I had _____ egg and _____ glass of milk for breakfast.

2. _____ leopard which escaped from _____ zoo has been caught.

3. Have you finished reading _____ book you borrowed last week?

4. Steve has _____ terrible headache.

5. _____ event like this happens only once a year.

6. _____ rabbit was hiding in the bush. When we went near the bush, _____ rabbit ran away.

7. _____ girl you met is the class topper.

8. Can you give me _____ glass of water?

9. Who spilt ink on _____ carpet?

10. _____ oval is shaped like _____ egg.

C Complete the following sentences with A, AN or THE:

1. Danny wanted _____ new bicycle for Christmas.
   (a) A   (b) AN   (c) THE

2. Jennifer tasted _____ birthday cake her mother had made.
   (a) A   (b) AN   (c) THE

3. The children have _____ new teacher called Mr. Green.
   (a) A   (b) AN   (c) THE

4. All pupils must obey _____ rules.

(a) A   (b) AN   (c) THE

5. Dad turned on _____ radio to listen to _____ news.

(a) A   (b) AN   (c) THE

6. Alex is in Boston studying for _____ MBA.

(a) A   (b) AN   (c) THE

7. The teacher read _____ interesting article from the newspaper.

(a) A   (b) AN   (c) THE

8. There was _____ huge crowd of people outside the church.

(a) A   (b) AN   (c) THE

9. Julie talked for _____ hour about her school project.

(a) A   (b) AN   (c) THE

10. _____ European expert was invited to speak to the committee.

(a) A   (b) AN   (c) THE

11. India is _____ largest democracy in the world.

(a) A   (b) AN   (c) THE

12. It was _____ unforgettable experience.

(a) A   (b) AN   (c) THE

PRONOUNS

Look at these pictures and read the words aloud.

He is eating an ice-cream.

It is a cat.

They are girls.

In sentence 1, the word 'He' is used for a boy.

In sentence 2, the word 'It' is used for a cat.

In sentence 3, the word 'They' is used for the girls.

'They', 'It' and 'He' are words used in the place of Nouns.
Words that we use in place of nouns are called Pronouns.

26

He	It	She	They

1. _____ is a blue bag.

2. _____ is a joker.

3. _____ are bananas.

4. _____ is my grandmother.

5. _____ is a small dog.

Look at these pictures and read the words aloud.

 **I**

(One)

 **We**

(Many)

 **You**

(One)

 **You**

(Many)

 **He**

(One boy)

 **She**

(One girl)

 **She**

(One)

 **It**

(Many)

B Put 'one' or 'many' for each of the pronouns.

1. He   –   _____

2. They   –   _____

3. It   –   _____

4. She   –   _____

5. I   –   _____

6. We   –   _____

Let's Do

C Who Am I?

Hi! My name is Ryan.

I / He _____ am 6 years old.

I have a brother.

I / He _____ is 8 years old.

I have a sister.

I / She _____ is 10 years old.

My father goes to office.

I / He _____ is a doctor.

29

My mother's name is Reni.

I / She _____ is very nice.

My mother and father take care of us.

He / They _____ love us very much.

D Circle the correct pronoun.

1.   They / I are going to school.

2.   It / He is a bat.

3.   She / They are my friends.

4.   You / He is my father.

5.   I / They am a girl.

6.   We / I are eating oranges.

7.   It / They is cold.

8.   She / You are a doctor.

9.   You / It is a new dress.

10.   I / She have a doll.

E **Rewrite the sentences using pronouns in place of words in colour.**

1. This is my sister. My sister has a dog.

    This is my sister. She has a dog.
    _____

2. This is my uncle. My uncle is a shopkeeper.

    _____ .

3. This is my brother. My brother plays football.

    _____ .

4. My brother and my sister help me. My brother and my sister are helpful.

    _____ .

5. The flowers are pink. The flowers look lovely.

    _____ .

6. I live in Delhi. Delhi is a big city.

    _____ .

7. The elephant has a trunk. The elephant is big.

    _____ .

8. The stars are bright. The stars are twinkling.

    _____ .

ADJECTIVES

Animals in the zoo

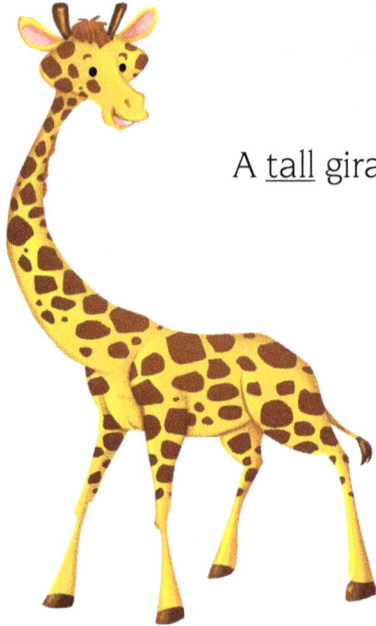

A <u>tall</u> giraffe

A <u>big</u> elephant

A <u>heavy</u> hippopotamus

Do you see the underlined words <u>tall</u>, <u>big</u> and <u>heavy</u>?

These words tell you about the shape and size of the animals. These describing words are called **adjectives**.

> **An adjective is a word that tells more about a noun or a pronoun. In other words, it is a word that describes a person, animal, place, or thing.**

> **ADJECTIVES are called DESCRIBING WORDS.**

HAPPY

SMALL

TASTY

COLD

FAST

SOFT

> **Adjectives tell the quality of people, things, places and objects.**

**Match the following adjectives with the correct object/
people.**

Adjective	Object/people
1. Pretty	
2. Old	
3. Clean	
4. Cold	
5. Funny	

Read the words given in the boxes below.

COLOUR

red	brown	orange
yellow	green	white
pink	purple	blue
violet	silver	black
golden		

SHAPE

square	round	oval
flat	narrow	deep
broad	rectangle	

SIZE

small	tiny	huge
big	medium	large
tall	short	little
fat	thin	

Adjectives tell the COLOUR, SHAPE and SIZE of people, things, places and objects.

B **Circle the adjectives (shape, size, and colour).**

1. There is a red apple.

2. The boy is tall.

35

3. I have a small car.

4. The girl has a pink bag.

5. This is a big rock.

6. I saw a yellow flower.

7. A tiny bird is sitting.

8. I ate a large burger.

9. The car is black.

10. The way is narrow.

Find out how many?

Two children

One flower

Five turtles

The underlined words are also adjectives as they tell the quantity of children, flowers and turtles.

> **Adjectives also describe the number of people, things, places and objects.**

C **Fill in the blanks with the correct adjectives (numbers).**

1. Human have _____ fingers.

2. We have _____ eyes.

3. There are _____ eggs in a dozen.

4. The traffic light has _____ colours.

5. A spider has _____ legs.

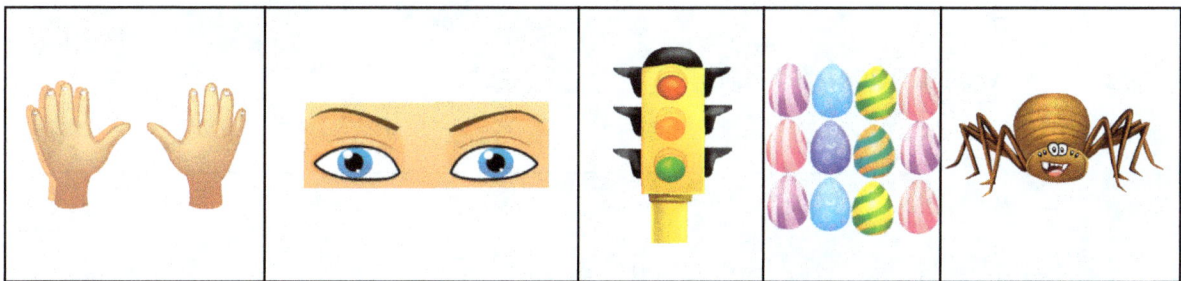

Let's Revise

Adjectives describe the quality, colour, shape, size, and number of nouns and pronouns in a sentence.

Quality	Colour	Shape	Size	Number
Dirty	Yellow	Square	Big	Five
Cute	Pink	Round	Small	Two
Hot	Blue	Oval	Fat	Three
Young	Grey	Star	Tall	One
Strong	White	Rectangular	Wide	Twenty

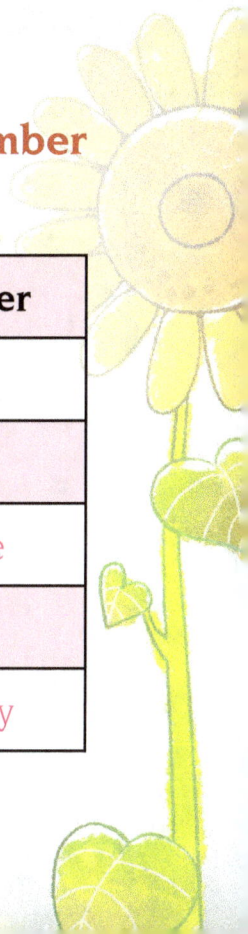

D **Re-write the sentences after adding the adjectives. The first one is done as an example.**

1. That is a glass.

   Ans. That is a big glass. _____

2. There was a dog.

   Ans. _____

3. My father has a car.

   Ans. _____

4. The boys are playing with a ball.

   Ans. _____

5. The man is eating bananas.

   Ans. _____

E **Find out the age!**

1. I am _____ years old.

2. My mother is _____ years old.

3. My sister is _____ years old.

4. My grandmother is _____ years old.

5. My friend is _____ years old.

F **From the box given below, choose all the adjectives from this word mat and write them down in the blank box.**

BRIGHT	DELHI	SAD	FROG
LAZY	BUS	GOOD	EMPTY
YOUNG	SEVEN	BRAVE	BOY
CYCLE	ROUND	APPLE	TINY
RED	PLAY	BAD	LION
SMALL	TASTY	MILK	BLACK
BOOK	PLANE	WATERMELON	TEN

Read the story and circle all the adjectives.

The Brown Bear Story

Once upon a time, there was a little boy whose name was Sam. On his birthday, his father and mother got him a soft brown teddy bear. It was small. Sam was happy and carried his cute bear with him everywhere he went. At night, Sam always slept next to the toy bear.

The brown bear was his favourite toy. Sam took the cute bear to the park to play. He showed it to his friends. His friends liked the small bear very much.

One day, Sam could not find his brown teddy bear. He asked his mom and dad, and he looked for his toy bear everywhere but could not find it. Sam became very sad and started missing his teddy.

After a few days, when Sam was arranging his room, he saw the brown teddy bear under a pile of clothes.

Sam was very happy when he found out about his best friend, the brown bear.

Position of Adjectives

Descriptive adjectives tell us more about the size, shape, colour, texture and condition of a noun.

Example:

- I don't like **sticky** rice.
- That is a **pretty** dress.
- Ben has a **huge** dog.

Position of adjectives

Adjective usually comes **before** the noun it describes, but sometimes it can come **after** the noun (or a pronoun), later in the sentence.

Before a noun:

- Today is a **cold** day.

After a noun:

- He needs someone **talented** to do this job.

A Circle the most suitable adjective in brackets for each sentence.

1. The (blunt, sharp) knife sliced the bread easily.

2. The (clean, dirty) laundry was piled up on the floor.

3. John is a (brilliant, small) student.

4. Maria put her (tired, small) feet in hot water.

5. Our (gentle, ferocious) dog bared its teeth at the intruder.

6. She is my (good, poor) friend.

7. We saw a (green, big) elephant in the zoo.

8. The players were upset by the (hostile, big) crowd.

9. Nancy heard a (strange, hard) sound in the night.

10. Bob heard a (loud, faint) cry coming from a great distance.

B **Underline the adjectives in these sentences. Write the noun described by each adjective in the box.**

1. Molly went for a long walk.   _____

2. Spanish is a difficult language to learn.   _____

3. All the clothes drying in the sun are wet.   _____

4. The witch was a bad woman.   _____

5. Wish you have a safe journey.   _____

6. My father is a tall man.   _____

7. The soldiers were brave.   _____

8. John is my good friend.   _____

9. The mischievous monkeys are jumping all over the fence.   _____

10. The giant lived in a beautiful garden.   _____

> Many nouns can be changed into adjectives by adding a **suffix**
> such as: **-y, -ful, -less, ish, -ly, -some, -ed, -ing, -able, -al, -ant,**
> **-ar, -ary, -ent, -ic, -id, -ive, -ous.**

Example:

sleep - sleepy; success - successful; pity - pitiless; whole - wholesome, etc.

C Change the nouns given below into adjectives. The first one is done for you.

nation	national	boy	_____
love	_____	knowledge	_____
gloom	_____	music	_____
awe	_____	comfort	_____
fool	_____	grace	_____
fear	_____	juice	_____
sleeve	_____	reverse	_____
child	_____	arm	_____
home	_____	danger	_____
quarrel	_____	rot	_____

D Complete the following sentences by choosing the appropriate adjective from the clue box given below.

| windy | active | barking | costly | forgetful |
| frightening | broken | curly | stolen | interesting |

1. Sara has nice _____ hair.

2. My grandmother has become very _____ after her accident.

3. A _____ dog at night is very annoying.

43

1. This looks like an _____ movie.

2. Tom is an _____ child.

3. Chicago is a _____ city.

4. The thief tried to sell the _____ watches.

5. It is _____ to buy a penthouse.

6. They had a _____ experience last night.

7. Don't sit on the _____ chair.

VERBS

Look at these pictures and read the words aloud.

SLEEP

SING

READ

EAT

KICK

CLEAN

The words **eat, sleep, kick, clean, sing and read** are action words.

A **verb** is a word that shows actions.

All doing words are called **verbs**.

A **What are they doing? Circle the right word.**

The father is _____.

Reading / Sleeping

The bird is _____.

Flying / Eating

Zeba is _____ on a chair.

Sitting / Standing

The baby is _____ milk.

Playing / Drinking

Rohan is _____.

Singing / Writing

Daily Routine
Everyday actions are Verbs.

B **Put your daily routines actions in order by drawing lines.**

Now write the names of these activities in order.

1. _____   2. _____   3. _____

4. _____   5. _____

| BRUSHING | BATHING | EXERCISING |
| GETTING UP | EATING | BREAKFAST |

47

C **Complete the sentences below using verbs that show daily routine.**

1. I _____ at 7:00 a.m.

2. I _____ a shower at 7:15 a.m.

3. I _____ my breakfast every morning.

4. I _____ the bus at 8:00 a.m.

5. I _____ to God every day.

6. I _____ a bicycle for 2 hours.

7. I _____ with my friends at 5:00 p.m.

8. I _____ milk twice a day.

9. I _____ my homework daily.

10. I _____ my mother in the kitchen.

11. I _____ a book in the evening.

12. I _____ television for one hour.

13. I _____ my dinner at 9:00 p.m.

14. I _____ to bed at 10:00 p.m.

Types of Verbs

A verb can be categorised as one of the following:

Action Verb

An **action verb** is a verb that **conveys action**.

Example:

- The dog **chases** the cat.
- A spider **spins** a web.

Action verbs are of two kinds:

1. Transitive Verb

A transitive verb is an action verb that acts on something (i.e., it has a direct object).

Example:

- He **writes** books.

(Here, the direct object is a book.)

- Lee **answers** all the questions.

(Here, the direct object is the **questions**.)

The direct object of a transitive verb can be found by finding the verb and asking "what?"

2. Intransitive Verb

An intransitive verb is an action verb that does not act on something (i.e., there is no direct object).

Example:

- The rain **fell**.

- My throat **hurts**.

Sometimes a preposition comes after an intransitive verb, followed by the object.

My friend **works** in (preposition) a bank (object).

John **lives** near (preposition) the stadium (object).

> Some verbs such as **meet, play sing, sleep, write** can be both **transitive and intransitive**.

Stative Verb

> **A stative verb** expresses a **state** rather than an action. A stative verb typically relates to a **state of being, a thought, or an emotion**.

Example:

- I **am** at home.

- She **believes** in fairies.

- He **feels** sad.

Auxiliary Verb

> **An auxiliary verb** (or helping verb) accompanies a **main verb** (action verb). It express either tense or voice. The most common auxiliary verbs are **be, do, and have** (in their various forms).

Examples:

- Harry **has** eaten all the candies.

(Here **has** helps to express **tense**.)

- The table **has been** prepared.

(Here **has been** help to express **voice** (in this case, the passive voice).

A **Fill in the blank with the correct auxiliary verb from the choices presented:**

1. What _____ the kids doing when you last saw them? (was, were, are, did, been)

2. Maria _____ always wanted to do paragliding. (was, doesn't, has, is, have)

3. Terry_____ writing an e-mail to a client at the moment. (was, has, is, have)

4. Carl _____ want to go to the movies; he wants to play video games. (doesn't, isn't, wasn't, hasn't)

5. There _____ no news update about the latest plane crash. (are, were, do, is)

6. I _____ ten dollars now. (has, have, are, had)

7. Where _____ you go on your summer vacation? (were, been, are, did, does)

8. There _____ a rose bush in the garden untill last year. (was, is, have, are)

9. Steve _____ going to be upset when he hears what happened. (will, don't, is, didn't, has)

10. I really like fish, but I _____ care for meat. (weren't, been, don't, is, was)

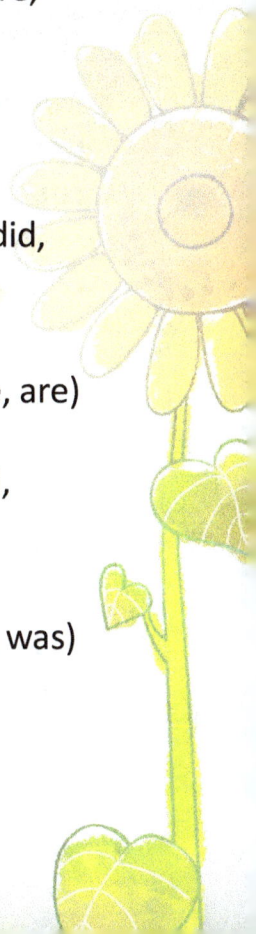

B **Underline the correct word in the brackets in each sentence.**

1. The cake you made yesterday (is, are, was) delicious.

2. If he (didn't, don't, doesn't) arrive on time, he'll have to take a later flight.

3. A spider (has, had, is) eight legs.

4. We (did, do, does) mental sums every day.

5. Good friends (do, does, are) things together.

6. Today I (had, has, have) $2 in my pocket.

7. Dad (had been, have been, has been) working hard all day.

8. There (were, was had) floods when the dam burst last year.

9. Sarah (don't, isn't, doesn't) ski or roller skate.

10. (Did, Has, Had) Sarah bring juice?

Modal Verb

A modal verb is a type of auxiliary verb used to express functions such as **ability, possibility, permission, or an obligation.** The modal auxiliary verbs are **can, could, may, might, must, ought to, shall, should, will, and would.**

Examples:

- Harry **can** eat a lot of candies.
  (Here **can** helps to express **ability**.)

- Harry **might** eat that candy before he gets home.
  (Here **might** helps to express **possibility**.)

- Harry **may** eat as many candies as he likes.
  (Here **may** helps to express **permission**.)

C **Fill in the blanks with appropriate modal auxiliary verbs.**

1.   My grandmother is eighty-five, but she _____ still read and write without glasses.

2.   _____ I come with you?

3.   _____ you help me with the housework, please?

4.   There was a time when I _____ stay up very late.

5.   _____ I sit with you?

6.   You _____ stop when the traffic lights turn red.

7.   It is snowing outside so I _____ stay at home.

8.   I _____ get you a shawl from Kashmir.

9.   _____ you mind if I borrowed your car?

10. _____ you take care of my dog for a day?

11. I _____ to help mother with the housework.

12. She _____ sell her home because she needs money.

STORY TIME
BORN TO BE A BUTTERFLY

A butterfly <u>lays</u> eggs.

An egg <u>hatches</u>.

A caterpillar <u>comes</u> out.

The caterpillar <u>turns</u> into a pupa.

The caterpillar <u>changes</u> inside the pupa.

A butterfly <u>comes</u> out of the pupa.

The butterfly <u>lays</u> eggs again.

The butterfly <u>dies</u>.

All the underlined words in the story are VERBS.

Life Cycle of a Butterfly

Pupa

Caterpillar

Butterfly

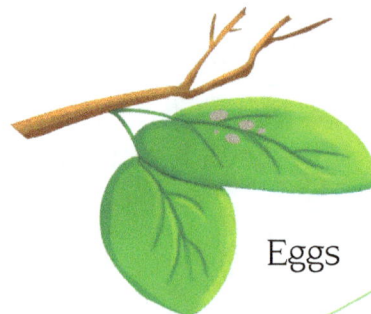
Eggs

Let's Revise

A verb is a doing or action word

LAUGH	JOG	DRAW	RUN
PLAY	CRY	SING	DANCE
COOK	SWIM	TALK	DO

Let's Do

A Fill in the blanks using verbs. Choose from the box below.

eat	play	clap	wash
drink	stand	write	sleep

1. I _____ with my toys.

2. We _____ with our hands.

3. I _____ my face in the morning.

4. I _____ on my bed.

5. I _____ fruits.

6. We _____ with a pencil.

7. I _____ milk.

8. We _____ on our feet.

B Fill in the blanks with actions that people do. Choose from the box below.

Paint	Repair	Teach	Drive
Fly	Help	Love	Clean

1. All drivers _____ cars.

2. The teachers _____ children.

3. All cobblers _____ shoes.

4. All sweepers _____ the rooms.

5. The pilots _____ the planes.

6. The painters _____ the pictures.

7. The policemen _____ the people.

8. Our parents _____ us.

C Write three of your favourite verbs. Draw pictures in the space given and make a sentence with each of them. Follow the given example.

VERB   PICTURE

READ

SENTENCE – They read a book.

1.

SENTENCE – _____

2.

SENTENCE – _____

3.

SENTENCE – _____

4.

SENTENCE – _____

OVERVIEW 1

A.   **Read the following words. Write (P) for people (Pl) for places and (T) for things.**

book ( )   rock ( )   water ( )   market ( )
baby ( )   teacher ( )   woman ( )   tree ( )
cloud ( )   garden ( )   brother ( )   friend ( )
computer ( )   policeman ( )   house ( )   office ( )
singer ( )   pencil ( )   guitar ( )   John ( )

OVERVIEW 2

B.   **Underline all the adjectives that describe you and use these in the sentences.**

quiet	loud	young	old	funny	bright	short
tall	silly	shy	happy	grumpy	cheerful	sporty

1.   I am 6 years old. I am _____.

2.   In the morning, I feel _____.

3.   My friends laugh at my jokes and say that I am _____.

4.   Today, I am in a _____ mood.

5.   I like to wear _____ outfits.

OVERVIEW 3

C.   Today, we went to the zoo. The first thing we saw was a _____ (colour) _____ (animal) _____ ing (action word). The zookeeper told us that it was _____ (number) years old. It was very _____ (size). It had a ____ (size) ____ (body part). We also saw other animals such as _____, _____, and _____.(names)

OVERVIEW 4

D. We are DOING WORDS. We all end with 'ing'.

1. I am having a pizza. I am E __ T __ __ __.
2. I am not awake. I am S L __ __ __ I N G.
3. I am not standing. I am S __ T __ I __ __.
4. I have a book. I am R __ A __ I N __.
5. I am having milk. I am D R __ __ __ I N G.
6. The plates are dirty. I am C L __ __ __ I N G them.

E. We are colours. We describe words.

1. The apple is __ __ __.
2. The sun is __ __ __ __ __ __.
3. Snow is __ __ __ __ __.
4. Grass is __ __ __ __ __.
5. The sky is __ __ __ __.
6. Wood is __ __ __ __ __.

OVERVIEW 5

F. Read each sentence. Choose the correct pronoun that can replace the underlined word(s) in each sentence.

1. Rose is writing a report on Graham Bell.
   a. Them   b. Her   c. It   d. She
2. My brother and I are going.
   a. Them   b. It   c. Her   d. We
3. The piano is mine.
   a. Them   b. It   c. Her   d. We
4. An ice cream truck drove near my house.
   a. it   b. They   c. her   d. him
5. James completed his homework.
   a. her   b. He   c. they   d. them

ANSWER KEY

The English Alphabet

(C)

tap	sun	owl
cap	dog	ten
nip	lip	ant
bun	mug	red
hen	cow	gun
pin	van	bed
bird	jump	bull
bowl	clap	pick

(D)
- Alligator
- Buffalo
- Crocodile
- Duck
- Hen
- Lion
- Sheep
- Zebra
- Bird
- Cat
- Dog
- Frog
- Horse
- Pig
- Tiger

Nouns

(A)
1. Soni
2. Robby
3. Sam
4. Danny
5. Nancy

(B) Fruits, Cereals, Bread, Milk
Books, Pencils, Pens, Lunch-Box
Car, Train, Bus, Aeroplane, Cycle
T-Shirt, Shorts, Frock, Suit

(C)
1. Park
2. School
3. Shop
4. Hospital
5. Library

(D)
1. Cow
2. Giraffe
3. Hen
4. Tiger
5. Cat
6. Dog
7. Elephant
8. Lion
9. Octopus
10. Duck

(E)
1. Apples
2. Balls
3. Plates
4. Frogs
5. Books
6. Trees
7. Houses
8. Toys
9. Bags
10. Birds

Countable Nouns and Uncountable Nouns

(A)

Countable	Uncountable
Carrots	Broccoli
Tomatoes	Rice
Potatoes	Cheese
Apples	Milk
Strawberries	Chocolate
Cherries	Soup

(B)
1. Cereals
2. Hair
3. Money
4. Salt
5. Milk
6. Air
7. Smoke
8. Luggage
9. Health
10. Electricity

(C)
1. some
2. a and a
3. an and a
4. some
5. some
6. a
7. an
8. some
9. an
10. a

(D)

Children	Countable
Hair	Uncountable
Noise	Countable
Paper	Uncountable
Rooms	Countable
Room	Uncountable
Bottles	Countable
Butter	Uncountable
Time	Uncountable
Polticians	Countable
Milk	Uncountable
Clay	Uncountable
Instruments	Countable
Cookies	Countable

Revision

(A)

Cat	House	Book
Tree	Car	

Lunch	Foot	Apple
Cow	Pan	Dog
Hand		

(B)
1. Pencil
2. Book
3. Pig
4. Table
5. Bus
6. Finger
7. Monkey
8. Ball
9. Song
10. Room

Articles

(A)
1. a and the
2. the
3. an
4. a
5. a
6. the
7. the and the
8. an
9. the
10. a

(B)
1. an and a
2. the
3. the
4. a
5. An
6. A and the
7. The
8. a
9. the
10. An and an

(C)
1. a
2. the
3. a
4. the
5. the and the
6. an
7. an
8. a
9. an
10. a
11. the
12. an

Pronouns

(A)
1. It
2. He
3. They
4. She
5. It

(B)
1. One
2. Many
3. One
4. One
5. One
6. Many

(C)
1. I
2. He
3. She
4. He
5. She
6. They

(D)
1. They
2. It
3. They
4. He
5. I
6. We
7. It
8. You
9. It
10. I

(E)
2. This is my uncle. He is a shopkeeper.
3. This is my brother. He plays football.
4. My brother and my sister help me. They are helpful.
5. The flowers are pink. They look lovely.
6. I live in Delhi. It is a big city.
7. The elephant has a trunk. It is big.
8. The stars are bright. They are twinkling.

Adjectives

(A)
1. Pretty Princess
2. Old man
3. Clean Room
4. Cold Ice-cream
5. Funny Clown

(B)
1. There is a red apple.
2. The boy is tall
3. I have a small car.
4. The girl has a pink bag.
5. This is a big rock.
6. I saw a yellow flower.
7. A tiny bird is sitting.
8. I ate a large burger.
9. The car is black.
10. The way is narrow.

(C)
1. Human have __five__ fingers
2. We have _two____ eyes.
3. There are ____twelve__ eggs in a dozen.
4. The traffic light has _____ three___ colours.
5. A spider has __eight___ legs.

(D)
2. There was a big dog.
3. My father has a black car.
4. The boys are playing with a blue ball.
5. The man is eating five bananas.

(F)
Bright, sad, Lazy, good, empty, young, seven, ten, brave, round, tiny, red, bad, small, black, tasty.

(G)
Once upon a time, there was a little boy, his name was Sam. On his birthday, father and mother got him a soft brown teddy bear. It

was small. Sam was happy and carried his cute bear with him everywhere he went. At night Sam always slept next to the toy bear.

The brown bear was his favourite toy. Sam took the cute bear to the park to play. He showed it to his five friends. His friends liked the lovely bear very much.

One day, Sam could not find his brown teddy bear. He asked his mom, his dad and looked for his toy bear everywhere but could not find it.

Sam became very sad and started missing his teddy.

After a few days, when Sam was arranging his room, he saw the brown teddy bear under a pile of clothes.

Sam was very happy when he found out his best friend, the brown bear.

Position of Adjectives

(A)
1.	sharp	2.	dirty
3.	brilliant	4.	tired
5.	ferocious	6.	good
7.	big	8.	hostile
9.	strange	10.	faint

(B)
Adjectives	Noun
long	walk
difficult	language
wet	clothes
bad	woman
safe	journey
tall	man
brave	soldiers
good	friend
mischievous	monkeys
beautiful	garden

(C)
nation - national	love - lovely
gloom - gloomy	awe - awesome
fool - foolish	fear - fearful
sleeve - sleeveless	child - childlike
home - homely	quarrel - quarrelsome
boy - boyish	knowledge - knowledgeable
music - musical	comfort - comfortable

grace - graceful	juice - juicy
reverse - reverse	arm - armless
danger - dangerous	rot - rotten

(D)
1.	curly	2.	forgetful
3.	barking	4.	interesting
5.	active	6.	windy
7.	stolen	8.	costly
9.	frightening	10.	broken

Verbs

(A)
1.	Reading	2.	Flying
3.	Sitting	4.	Drinking
5.	Writing		

(B)
1.	Getting up	2.	Brushing
3.	Exercising	4.	Bathing
5.	Eating Breakfast		

(C)
1. I get up at 7:00 a.m.
2. I take a shower at 7:15 a.m.
3. I eat my breakfast every morning.
4. I take the bus at 8:00 a.m.
5. I pray to God every day.
6. I ride a bicycle for 2 hours
7. I play with my friends at 5:00 p.m.
8. I drink milk twice a day.
9. I complete my homework daily.
10. I help my mother in the kitchen.
11. I read a book in the evening.
12. I watch television for one hour.
13. I eat my dinner at 9:00 p.m.
14. I go to bed at 10:00 p.m

Types of Verbs

(A)
1.	were	2.	has
3.	is	4.	doesn't
5.	is	6.	have
7.	did	8.	was
9.	is	10.	don't

(B)
1.	was	2.	doesn't
3.	has	4.	do
5.	do	6.	have
7.	has been	8.	were
9.	doesn't	10.	Did

(C)
1. can
2. can
3. could
4. could
5. may
6. must
7. will
8. will
9. would
10. will
11. ought
12. might

Revision

(A)
1. Play
2. Clap
3. Wash
4. Sleep
5. Eat
6. Write
7. Dink
8. Stand

(B)
1. Drive
2. Teach
3. Repair
4. Clean
5. Fly
6. Paint
7. Help
8. Love

Overview 1

A.

People	Places	Things
Singer	Garden	Book
Teacher	House	Computer
Baby	Office	Cloud
Brother	Market	Tree
Friend		Water
John		Pencil
Woman		Guitar
Policeman		Rock

Overview 2

B.
1. Young
2. Cheerful
3. Funny
4. Happy
5. Sporty

Overview 3

C.
1. Black
2. Elephant
3. Sitting
4. Five
5. Small
6. Big
7. Trunk
8. Giraffe
9. Zebra
10. Lion

Overview 4

D.
1. EATING
2. SLEEPING
3. SITTING
4. READING
5. DRINKING
6. CLEANING

E.
1. Red
2. Yellow
3. White
4. Green
5. Blue
6. Brown

Overview 5

F.
1. She
2. We
3. It
4. It
5. He

WORK SPACE

www.ingramcontent.com/pod-product-compliance
Lightning Source LLC
LaVergne TN
LVHW081336060426
835513LV00014B/1315